Wildfire Rescue

Take a book
leave a book

Written by
Rekha S. Rajan

Illustrated by
Courtney Lovett

BRANCHES™

SCHOLASTIC INC.

To Katie Heit, for being an incredible editor and friend—RSR

For my family, my beautiful disaster squad—CL

During any disaster, please make sure to follow instructions from trusted adults.

Text copyright © 2024 by Rekha S. Rajan
Illustrations © 2024 by Courtney Lovett

Library of Congress Cataloging-in-Publication Data
Names: Rajan, Rekha S., author. | Lovett, Courtney, illustrator.
Title: Wildfire rescue / written by Rekha S. Rajan ; illustrated by Courtney Lovett.
Description: First edition. | New York : Scholastic, 2024. | Series: Disaster squad ; 1 | Audience: Ages 6–8 | Audience: Grades 2–3 | Summary: The Jackson family, including eight-year-old Jaden and his sister, Leela, travel the United States responding to disasters, helping people and rescuing animals—but they have never responded to a wildfire like the one raging in Northern California.
Identifiers: LCCN 2022058824 | ISBN 9781338828832 (paperback) | ISBN 9781338828849 (hardback)
Subjects: LCSH: Wildlife rescue—Juvenile fiction. | Animal rescue—Juvenile fiction. | Wildfires—Juvenile fiction. | California, Northern—Juvenile fiction. | CYAC: Wildlife rescue—Fiction. | Animal rescue—Fiction. | Wildfires—Fiction. | California, Northern—Fiction. Classification: LCC PZ7.1.R3456 Wi 2023 | DDC 813.6 [Fic] —dc23/eng/20230508
LC record available at https://lccn.loc.gov/2022058824

ISBN 978-1-338-82884-9 (hardcover) / ISBN 978-1-338-82883-2 (paperback)

10 9 8 7 6 5 4 3 2 1   24 25 26 27 28

Printed in India   197
First edition, August 2024
Edited by Katie Heit
Book design by Jaime Lucero

Table of Contents

Meet the Jackson Family!

Leela

Jaden

Lucky

Lamar (Dad)

Jaya (Mom)

Dust Storm

"**G**et out of my way!" Jaden Jackson yelled as he plopped onto the sofa with a THUD! "This is the coziest RV to travel around the country in."

"Do you have to yell and jump *all the time*?" His older sister, Leela, rolled her eyes as she put a bag of popcorn in the microwave.

Their dog, Lucky, wagged her furry tail and lifted her pointy ears at the sound of the POP, POP, POP!

It was Friday afternoon. The Jackson family was at a campsite in Nebraska. It was going to be a relaxing weekend making s'mores and grilling hot dogs.

"I cannot wait until I can drive the RV," Jaden said.

"You're only eight! That is too young to drive a recreational vehicle!" Mom laughed.

Just then, the phone rang. Everyone froze as Mom answered it.

Whenever the phone rang, it meant DISASTER!

When the phone rang, the Jackson family packed up their RV and went to help families facing a natural disaster.

Everyone had a very important role:

Mom was a famous journalist who took pictures and wrote news articles.

Dad was an award-winning doctor who helped people all over the world.

Jaden and Leela saved animals in danger.

Lucky helped, too . . . if she wasn't napping.

"Gimme the popcorn!" Jaden yanked on the bag Leela had just pulled from the microwave.

Buttery popcorn burst everywhere! Lucky crunched the pieces on the floor.

"Kiddos . . . " Mom said, hanging up the phone. Her voice was low and strong.

That meant no more funny business.

"We're going to a farm in Kansas," Mom continued. "There is a massive dust storm on its way there." She showed the location on her phone to Dad. He nodded.

"We can reach that farm in thirty minutes," he said. "Everyone, buckle up!"

Jaden and Leela jumped into their seats and put on their seat belts. There was no time to waste.

As the RV hit the road, Jaden and Leela opened their tablets to research the dust storm.

"'A dust storm starts when high winds lift chunks of dirt from the ground!'" Leela read. "'You should find shelter inside a building.'"

"It can last up to an hour!" Jaden added.

As they drove, the sky turned gloomy, even though it was early afternoon.

Thick brown clouds of dust began to surround the RV. It looked like big bushes were chasing one another down the road.

Jaden and Leela put on their safety goggles and grabbed flashlights from their Disaster Squad Kits.

"There's the farm!" Leela pointed as they stopped.

A local television news crew was filming the storm. A farmer was filling buckets with water and carrying them inside the barn. Mom grabbed her camera, and Dad picked up his medical bag.

Dad pushed open the door of the RV. BAM!

Baby Goats

The door slammed back toward Dad.

"That wind is strong," Dad shouted. "Follow us to the barn!"

Mom and Dad ran outside.

Jaden jumped out of the RV.

Leela and Lucky ran out after him. Leela held Lucky's leash.

The swirling dust made everyone sneeze. Ah ... Ah ... Ah ... CHOO!

WHOOSH!

"Jaden?" Leela called out. It was hard to see and breathe. The air was dry. Dust was everywhere!

BLEET! BLEET!

"What was that?" Jaden asked.

Lucky barked and ran toward the sound, pulling her leash from Leela's hands.

"Lucky, wait!" Leela cried.

Jaden and Leela ran after Lucky.

"The farmer's baby goats are trapped in their pen!" Leela cried, spotting them. "We have to help them get to the barn safely!"

Jaden held the gate open as Leela and Lucky circled the baby goats.

The sky was getting darker, and they couldn't see the barn.

"How will we get there?" Leela asked.

"The flashlights!" Jaden remembered.

Leela and Jaden used their flashlights to make a path to the barn. The baby goats ran toward it. Lucky followed behind.

Jaden and Leela pushed the doors open together.

The baby goats ran past the people sheltering inside the barn and into an open stall.

"I was getting worried about both of you," Mom said as she finished taking pictures of the activity.

A tall man wearing a plaid shirt waved as Dad finished putting a bandage on his arm.

"I'm Mr. McConnell," the man said. "I'm thankful the local news team called and you all came so quickly!" The farmer gave Jaden and Leela each a fist bump. "You saved our baby goats! That makes you junior farmers." He handed them a stack of empty plastic buckets. "Junior farmers always need a plan to store extra water during a dust storm. Please take these buckets as a thank-you. You never know when you will need to conserve water."

Later, when the storm had passed, the Jackson family waved goodbye and climbed back into the RV. The day had been scary and exciting at the same time.

"We saved the baby goats!" Leela cheered.

"Who's ready for a vacation?" Dad laughed.

"Who's ready for bed?" Mom asked with a sigh.

Just then, the phone rang.

Fire Season

3

"**W**hat's the emergency?"

Everyone froze as Mom spoke on the phone.

When she nodded, they nodded.

When she shook her head, they shook their heads.

Lucky thumped her tail on the floor.

"Wildfires?" Mom asked.

"What's happening?" Jaden whispered loudly.

"Mom said wildfires! We've never helped during a fire." Leela hugged Lucky. Lucky put her paws in the air. Leela scratched Lucky's stomach.

"I'll spray that fire down!" Jaden said.

"Now you're a firefighter?" Leela raised her eyebrows.

"I can be a firefighter if I want to!" Jaden's voice got louder.

"Oh yeah?" Leela asked, "What would you do if—"

"Kiddos," Mom started to say as she hung up the phone.

Jaden and Leela turned to Mom.

Lucky stopped thumping her tail.

"You know when the phone rings—" Mom said.

"Disaster!" Jaden and Leela said at the same time. "Jinx! Double jinx. Triple jinx!"

"There is another disaster, and people need our help," Mom explained.

"Where?" Dad asked.

"Northern California," Mom answered. "There are three wildfires that just sparked."

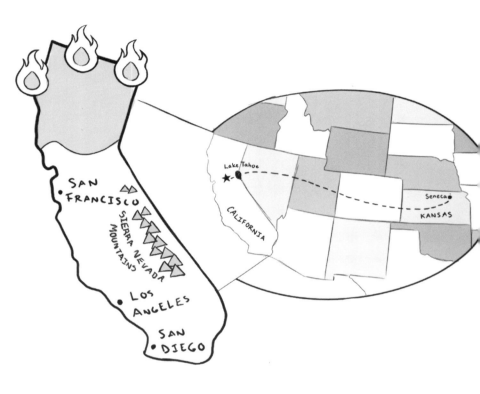

"It is fire season in California," Dad said.
"If there's a fire season," Jaden asked, "when is water season?"

"This is *not* a joke," Dad said. "In the summer, Northern California can reach over one hundred  degrees! The state is also in a drought. That means there is not enough rain, and the air and forests are dry. So wildfires are more likely to start and grow large very quickly."

"How do we stop a wildfire?" Leela asked.

"We don't. Firefighters do! But the fires spread fast," Mom said. "The smoke from these fires is already moving across the country."

"How far is California?" Leela asked.

"About two days of driving if we make quick stops," Dad said.

"Can we stop at Lake Tahoe? I can take a swim in that cool, blue water!" Jaden moved his arms in front of him, pretending to swim.

"We can't stop, but we'll drive by the lake," Dad replied. "We need to get to our destination quickly."

"Remember: Our goal is to help families and animals get to safety," Mom said.

"That's why we are the Disaster Quad!" Dad cheered and pumped his fist into the air.

"Daaaaad. Will you ever get it right? We are the Disaster *Squad* not Quad," Leela corrected. "*Quad* means four, and *Squad* means team! We can't forget the most important part of our team. Right, Lucky?"

Lucky barked.

WOOF!

"Got it. Disaster Squad," Dad said.

"Are we all packed up and ready to go?" Mom asked.

Dad shook his head. "Wait, that reminds me . . . SURPRISE!"

4

Night Vision

Dad pulled out two small boxes.

"It's not my birthday," Jaden said.

"Mine either," Leela added. "I'm not turning eleven yet."

"Anyone want to guess what's inside?" Mom asked.

"A phone?" Leela asked.

"A drone?" Jaden hoped.

Mom smiled and shook her head.

"You're both amazing helpers. We wanted to surprise you with a new item for your Disaster Squad Kits!" Dad said.

Every member of the Jackson family had their own Disaster Squad Kit. Each Disaster Squad Kit included:

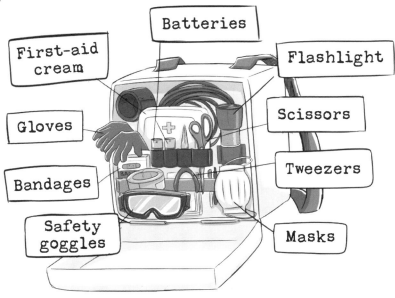

Dad gave one box to Jaden and one to Leela.

Jaden shook the box to hear what was inside.

Leela ripped open the wrapping.

"Wow!" Jaden gasped. "Night vision goggles! Cool!"

"Thanks!" Leela smiled.

"You can practice using them while we drive to California," Dad said.

As everyone buckled up, Dad slowly drove away from the barn. The blue lights inside the RV dimmed. It was dark outside.

Leela put three batteries into the goggles. The goggles looked like sunglasses, but they had a thick black strap and one long green lens. Leela adjusted the strap so they fit tightly around her head. With the goggles on, it was much easier to see in the dark!

"Everything looks neon green!" Jaden said.

"The box says we can see over twenty feet away!" Leela added.

As the RV drove down the road, Jaden and Leela peered out the windows.

"Night vision goggles will help you see better in the dark," Mom said.

"See anything exciting?" Dad asked.

Jaden turned his head slowly to the front of the RV. "Yeah! I see squirrels, an owl, and . . . HIT THE BRAKES!"

5

Turtle Trouble

SCREECH!

The RV slammed to a stop as Dad pulled quickly but safely to a to the side of the road.

"What's going on?" Dad asked Jaden.

"Look!" Jaden pointed out the windshield. "You can't see it because you don't have night vision goggles on."

"There's a turtle on the road!" Leela gasped, spotting it.

Dad turned the high-beam headlights on. A big, round shell was sitting in the middle of the road. A little head slowly poked out the front.

"It's so cute!" Leela said.

"Can we drive around it?" Jaden asked.

"What if someone else hits it?" Leela worried.

Dad nodded. "You're right. We should help it cross the road."

Mom put on her own night vision goggles. She opened the RV door and Leela followed her out.

"Lucky, you stay inside," Leela ordered.

Lucky barked. WOOF!

Dad pressed a button in the RV. The flashing red lights would tell other drivers there was an emergency.

Mom carefully walked toward the turtle and put several orange safety cones around the RV so other drivers would stop. The turtle pulled its head back inside its shell.

"Someone would have definitely hit it," Leela said. "It looks like a rock."

"Leela, gently hold the shell and the bottom when you pick it up," Mom said. "And wear gloves! Turtles have a bacteria that can make you sick if you don't handle them carefully."

"On it!" Leela said, heading back to the RV to get her Disaster Squad Kit. Dad and Jaden followed her back outside.

"I have a joke! Why did the turtle cross the road . . . " Dad started to say. Jaden groaned.

Leela pulled on plastic gloves from her Disaster Squad Kit and tightened her night vision goggles.

She crouched down next to the turtle and picked it up. The shell felt rough and bumpy. The bottom of the turtle felt slimy.

Mom, Dad, and Jaden shone flashlights onto the road in case there were other critters. This was an animal emergency.

Leela stood up with the turtle and slowly walked to the other edge of the highway. She gently placed the turtle in the grass. The turtle poked its head out, then pushed out its four feet to walk away.

"Woo-hoo!" Jaden cheered.

"No one wants to hear the end of my joke?" Dad asked.

"No, Dad!" Jaden and Leela said at the same time.

"Everyone back in the RV," Mom said. "Next stop, California!"

6

The Red Sky

Jaden opened his eyes.

"Wake up, sleepyhead," Mom said, gently shaking his arm. "We need to get going to the wildfire site."

Jaden climbed out of the top bunk bed and walked to the kitchen. "I'm hungry!" he said.

"You're always hungry." Leela giggled. She took a bite of her scrambled eggs and handed a piece of toast to Lucky.

Lucky munched on the toast.

"Do you notice anything about the sky?" Dad asked.

"Those clouds look really red!" Jaden said, grabbing a plate of bacon and eggs. "Is the sky on fire?"

"The sky turns red because of all the smoke," Mom said, pulling up examples on her phone. "The smoke particles are so strong, they scatter into the sky and absorb the blue color we usually see. This is called the red sky."

"Whoa," said Jaden.

"We've got to go. Everyone ready?" Dad asked.

Jaden and Leela sat at the small table in the kitchen and buckled up.

For the past two days, the Jackson family had driven from Kansas toward Northern California, only making stops at night.

"Where are the palm trees and beaches?" Jaden asked. "This place doesn't look like California."

"Southern California has palm trees. We are in Northern California, near the Sierra Nevada Mountains. Look!" Dad pointed to a large body of water to their right. "Do you know what that is?"

"A giant orange swimming pool?" Jaden guessed.

"It's Lake Tahoe," Mom said.

"Why is it orange?" Leela asked.

"It's from the smoke," Mom said. "The wildfires have made the beautiful blue lake look orange."

"How did the fires start?" Leela asked.

"Wildfires start in a lot of ways. When the weather gets very hot and there is no rain, it only takes a small spark to start a big fire. And one fire can create more fires," Mom explained.

"Like ten plus ten equals twenty fires?" Jaden asked.

"It's more like one small fire sends a hundred sparks, and then those sparks ignite new fires. Those small fires become big fires that cause a lot of damage," Dad said.

"Couldn't the rain put out the fires?" Jaden asked.

"Remember that California is in a drought," Mom said. "That means there hasn't been rain in weeks."

"Disaster Squad, take a deep breath," Dad said quietly as he pulled the RV to the side of the road where a meadow of grass that had already been burned was set up as a safe zone. "We're here."

Fire Chief Fran

CRACK! POP!

Flames burst into the sky.

Red lights were flashing.

Big gray hoses came out of the fire trucks. Firefighters aimed the nozzles as close to the fire as they safely could, spraying down the flames. Water blasted everywhere! Still, the fires didn't seem to be backing down.

"Those fire trucks are HUGE!" Jaden said.

Dad parked the RV.

A firefighter spotted them, waved, and started to walk over.

"Someone's coming!" Leela pointed.

Mom quickly opened the door. A gust of smoke blew into the RV as the firefighter stepped inside.

Jaden coughed.

Lucky sneezed.

"Hello!" the woman greeted them. "You must be the Jacksons. I am Fire Chief Fran. We're so happy to have your family here to help."

Jaden and Leela looked at the fire chief. Her bright yellow suit was stained with black patches. When she pulled off her safety goggles and mask, there were red marks on her face. Gray ash from the fires stuck to her everywhere.

"Nice to meet you," Dad said.

"How bad is it?" Mom pointed outside.

Fire Chief Fran sighed. "The fire spread quickly. In two days, these forest fires have already burned eighty-five thousand acres. That is equal to fifty thousand soccer fields."

"Wow!" Jaden gasped.

"There must be so many people who need help!" Dad said.

"And animals who might be trapped!" Leela worried.

"We're doing our best to contain the fire and save the forests," Fire Chief Fran said, "but we also need to make sure the families in the area can evacuate."

"What does 'evacuate' mean?" Jaden asked.

"To get out safely," Mom said. "Many people don't want to leave their homes and are scared of leaving important things behind."

"If I had to evacuate, I'd take my Disaster Squad Kit," Jaden said.

"If I had to evacuate, I'd take Lucky!" said Leela.

Lucky barked. WOOF!

"How can you see and breathe through all that smoke?" Jaden asked.

Fire Chief Fran wiped her goggles. "We have special gear: an oxygen tank we wear on our back and masks that cover our nose and mouth. We also measure the air quality using the air quality index, or AQI. Anything above an AQI of 150 is unhealthy to breathe."

"What is the AQI right now?" Leela asked.

"Right now it's 280. It is dangerous to breathe without a mask," Fire Chief Fran answered.

"How did the fire start?" Mom asked.

Fire Chief Fran frowned. "Two of the fires in the area started because of the heat and drought." She took a deep breath. "The third fire wasn't started by the weather. It was started . . . by a person."

8

Campfire Checklist

"**A** person did this?" Leela gasped.

Fire Chief Fran nodded. "The third fire was from a campfire that wasn't put out properly."

"That's so sad." Leela shook her head.

"There are over eighty fires burning in California," Fire Chief Fran said.

"EIGHTY?" Jaden shouted as he fell back onto the couch.

"Fire season used to last a few months here in the mountains. We did controlled burns of big areas below the trees to prevent even bigger fires from happening," Fire Chief Fran said. "But now, with the change in climate, California is hotter and drier than ever. Wildfires can start year-round."

"We camped in Yosemite last year," Leela said. "We made s'mores and Dad played the guitar! We didn't see wildfires then."

"Next time you go camping, remember the Campfire Checklist," Fire Chief Fran said. "We say, 'Camping is great if you follow these eight.' If you don't follow these tips, it could lead . . . to disaster."

Fire Chief Fran pulled a folded flyer from her pocket and handed it to Jaden and Leela. They read it together.

CAMPFIRE CHECKLIST

1. Follow campground rules.
2. Use a firepit.
3. Use a match to start the fire.
4. Add small twigs and watch the size of the fire.
5. Keep water ready in case the fire gets too big.
6. Watch the direction of the wind.
7. Don't ever leave the campfire!
8. Always put the fire out completely!

"Great fire tips," Jaden said.

"Now we need to go check on the families who need help and report on the damage," Mom said. "You two stay inside!"

"That's not fair!" Jaden argued. "We want to help! We drove so far, and —"

BOOM!

9

Water Drop!

"What WAS that loud boom?" Jaden asked.

Through the front window, they could see a huge tree lay across the road. Flames crackled and sparked from the branches.

"I asked for emergency air support so we can get this fire under control faster," Fire Chief Fran said. "We don't have enough water in the trucks to stop the fire."

ZOOM!

Three air tankers raced across the sky. When their bottom hatches opened, a thick red liquid poured through the air.

"Those air tankers are huge!" Leela gasped.

Fire Chief Fran nodded. "The liquid includes soap that helps the water stick to the leaves and stop the fires from spreading. The water from the trucks puts out the fires at the base of the trees."

Mom grabbed her camera and looked at Leela and Jaden. "Be safe, and wear your masks if you have to leave," she said.

Dad put on his safety gear, grabbed his medical bag, and followed Mom and Fire Chief Fran toward the fire trucks.

The fire roared. Thick smoke blanketed the trees. Sparks flew into the air like firecrackers.

One firefighter pulled out a big hose from the bottom of the fire truck. Another dragged the hose behind the lead firefighter, who sprayed gallons of water at the fire.

WHOOSH!

Jaden and Leela looked up. Jaden counted several helicopters flying in a line over the forest.

"There's more air support!" he cheered.

Each helicopter had a huge bag hanging from thick wires that released water over the burning trees.

Lucky barked and jumped at the door. WOOF! WOOF! *WOOF!*

"She sees something!" Leela said.

"I only see smoke." Jaden frowned.

"Look!" Leela pointed. "An animal is in trouble!"

10

Bear Cub

"**A** bear cub is trapped up in that tree!" Jaden said.

A brown bear cub was hanging on a large Sequoia tree. Smoke filled the air. The bear cub tried to climb higher, but the branches started to bend and sway in the strong wind.

Leaves burned and crumbled to the ground. The bear cub clung to the tree trunk with all four paws.

Lucky barked again. WOOF!

"I'm going to go help!" Jaden said.

"Me too!" Leela agreed.

Jaden and Leela fixed their safety goggles.

"Where are our masks?" Leela asked.

"Here!" Jaden grabbed two N95 masks from their Disaster Squad Kits.

The masks were snug. A little metal piece pinched the tops of their noses.

"Let's go!" Jaden said.

Leela touched the door of the RV. "The door and window feel warm," she warned. "We have to be careful."

Jaden pushed the door open. A huge gust of smoke blew into their faces. It felt like they were walking straight into a campfire, even though the fires were one hundred yards away.

"This smells like a bad barbecue!" Jaden coughed.

As they ran toward the edge of the forest, they could feel their skin getting warmer. Smoke circled them. Their safety goggles became foggy  as they looked up at the trapped cub.

"It's scared!" Jaden moved closer to the tree, trying to get a better look.

"Careful!" Leela shouted. "The mama bear could be close. And the fire is even closer!"

SNAP!

A tree branch fell to the ground. The bear cub's grip slipped as it slid down the tree trunk.

"The cub is falling!" Jaden yelled as he put his arms out in front of him.

"You can't catch a bear cub!" Leela cried.

CRACK!

Sparks exploded around Jaden and Leela. Another branch snapped off the tree and flew toward the ground.

"Jaden! WATCH OUT!" Leela screamed.

It was too late.

11

Make a Mask

"**N**O!" Leela screamed as a branch hit Jaden's arm.

With a thud, he fell to the ground.

"Jaden!" Leela ran toward her brother. Jaden lay on the ground next to several broken branches.

"Jaden?" Leela worried.

Jaden turned and coughed.

"Can you stand?" Leela said. "We have to get out of here!"

Leela put Jaden's arm around her neck to help him stand up. She glanced back and saw the bear cub had landed safely and was running into the forest.

Together, Jaden and Leela hurried back to the RV.

Inside, Jaden plopped down on the couch and ripped off his mask. Leela did the same. Lucky licked Jaden's hand.

"That was intense!" he said, rubbing his hurt arm.

The RV door burst open.

"What happened to you?" Dad demanded. "Didn't you hear me shouting your names?"

Leela shook her head.

"Dad! We just wanted to help the bear cub," Jaden said.

"That was dangerous," Dad scolded. "You don't try to touch animals that are trapped in a wildfire. The baby animals will eventually find their family." He opened his kit and put cream and a bandage on Jaden's arm.

Leela coughed. "Even with these masks, it tastes like I ate a burnt hot dog."

"It's a good thing you were wearing the N95 masks," Dad said. "They are stronger than bandannas or cloth masks."

Leela held her mask. It felt hard, like a piece of cardboard. "What if you don't have an N95?" she worried.

"You can always make a mask to protect you for a little while," Dad said. "Take two thick pieces of cloth and wet them before tying them around your nose and mouth."

"Why do you get them wet?" Jaden asked.

"The water helps stop the smoke from getting into your lungs," Dad said. "Try it."

Leela took a piece of cloth from the counter and dipped it in cold water from the kitchen sink. She held it over her mouth and nose. Her face was burning hot.

The cloth felt soft and cold.

"The fires are growing. People need food and supplies," Dad said.

Jaden and Leela put their N95 face masks back on.

Dad pushed open the RV door. "Disaster Squad, are you ready to help?"

12

Helping Out

"**W**here are we going?" Jaden asked.

Leela shrugged as they followed Dad toward a big tent.

"Mom is taking pictures of the fire and talking to the local news crew," Dad said. "You two can help out here."

Fire Chief Fran jogged toward them.

"Jacksons!" she said. "This is one of fifty stations where we pack and make safety kits. These kits are then taken to shelters in the state. Because the shelters get overcrowded, these stations help volunteers to be more efficient when making kits."

"What does 'efficient' mean?" Jaden asked.

"It means we are organized as a group and can make the kits faster," Fire Chief Fran replied. "Find a line to help make the safety kits. Each kit has a water bottle, a snack, wipes, a glow stick, first-aid cream, and bandages."

"Just like in our Disaster Squad Kits!" Jaden smiled.

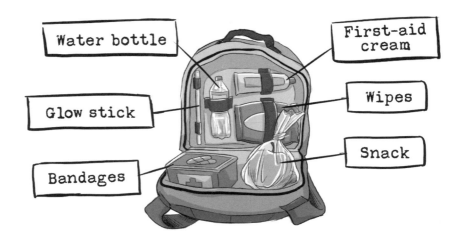

Water bottle

First-aid cream

Glow stick

Wipes

Bandages

Snack

"Stay safe," Dad said. "If anything happens, head to the RV. Mom and I will meet you there."

Dad ran toward a group of people sitting in an ambulance as Jaden and Leela followed Fire Chief Fran. Inside the tent, there were five rows of tables. Each table was filled with big stacks of items.

Leela counted nine people in the tent. Each person was wearing a mask.

"This is our assembly line," Fire Chief Fran said.

The corners of the tent shifted as the wind blew outside.

One person put a water bottle into a bag, then passed it to the next person, who put in a snack. The next person added wipes and a glow stick, and the last person added first-aid cream and bandages.

When the bag was full, it went into a big box and was loaded onto big moving trucks waiting outside.

Jaden and Leela stood at a table. Jaden put a bottle of water into a bag, then Leela put in a snack. She passed the bag to the next helper.

Everyone was working so fast!

"More water bottles here!"

"I need glow sticks!"

"This box is ready to go!"

People shouted across the tent.

Bags were tossed into boxes.

Boxes were tossed into trucks.

"Faster, Jaden," Leela said.

"I'm hungry," Jaden said.
"We missed lunch,
and those apples
look good."

"You are
always hungry."
Leela shook her
head.

Suddenly a siren
blared.

WOOOO!
WOOOO!

13

Evacuate

"**T**hat siren is so loud!" Jaden screamed as he covered his ears.

"I can't hear you!" Leela screamed back.

"EVACUATE! EVACUATE!" A loud voice boomed through a speaker. "Evacuate, now!"

Everyone in the tent hurried to clean up their work stations and evacuate.

"What's going on?" Leela worried.

Leela and Jaden put on their goggles and ran out of the tent. The smoke was getting thicker.

Fire Chief Fran ran over to them.

"A new fire has sparked. It is too hard to contain," she said. "Parts of the roads are blocked. You and your family need to evacuate."

"We have to get to the RV!" Jaden said.

"Hurry!" Fire Chief Fran said. "If we don't leave now, we could all be trapped."

The wind started to blow faster.

BAM!

Leela saw a giant tree branch slam into the outside of the tent. The sheet ripped in half.

They could see the trees crackling and sparking flames. Branches fell to the ground.

Leela grabbed a box full of finished kits and ran to the truck.

"Leela! We have to go!" Jaden yelled.

Leela tossed her box into the back of the truck. She held Jaden's hand as Fire Chief Fran guided them to the RV.

The lights on the fire trucks changed from yellow to red. Sirens blared!

WOOOO!

WOOOO!

WOOOO!

"There's so much smoke!" Jaden cried.

"Don't let go!" Leela said. "We are almost there."

Thick black smoke filled the air. Flames sprang up from the tops of the trees.

"Kids! Get in the RV!" Fire Chief Fran said, before she ran back to the tent.

"Where are Mom and Dad?" Jaden worried.

Leela pulled the door of the RV.

"The door is locked!" she cried out.

"How?" Jaden screamed. The sirens grew louder.

The warning sounded again.

"EVACUATE!"

Lucky jumped up and scratched at the window from the inside of the RV.

WOOF!

WOOF!

"Open the door, Lucky!" Leela yelled.

"She's a dog!" Jaden yelled back.

Lucky pawed at the door handle again and again.

The firefighters were climbing into their trucks. The tent was wrapped up and packed. Trucks were driving away.

"We're trapped here!" Leela cried, when suddenly they heard . . .

CLICK!

Traffic Jam

"**L**ucky opened the door!" Leela cheered as she climbed into the RV. Jaden jumped in behind her.

Lucky barked and wagged her long tail.

"What happened?" Mom asked.

Jaden and Leela turned to see Mom and Dad jumping into the RV. Mom pulled the door shut behind them.

Everyone took off their masks and goggles.

"Lucky saved us!" Jaden cheered.

"Smart dog." Dad smiled and started the engine.

"Where were you both?" Leela worried.

"We were right behind you. I know it was scary," Mom said.

Leela nodded. Tears dropped down her cheeks.

"Why do we need to evacuate?" Jaden asked.

"Three major highways are closed because of fallen trees and large fires. We need to get out while we can still drive on the last open highway," Mom said. "Everyone, buckle up."

Dad steered the RV down the road behind some of the fire trucks. Around them, trees burst into flames and smoke climbed into the air.

WHOOSH!

Air tankers dumped more water over the trees. Behind the RV, some of the flames started to sizzle and get smaller. The flaming red trees were starting to turn black.

"Where will we go?" Leela asked.

"To an emergency shelter," Mom said.

Leela looked around. Her family was covered with gray ash from the fires. Mom handed out cold water to drink and wet cloths so everyone could wipe their faces.

"I'm still hungry," Jaden said as he opened a box of cookies.

Leela looked at Jaden and giggled.

"What's so funny?" He frowned.

"You have burnt leaves stuck in your hair," she said.

Jaden shook his head from side to side. Crumpled leaves fell to the table.

"Uh-oh," Dad said after they'd been driving for a while.

"What's wrong?" Mom asked.

Ahead of their RV was a line of at least one hundred cars.

"We're in a traffic jam." Dad sighed.

"Fire Chief Fran helped everyone get away from the fires," Mom said.

Leela hugged Lucky. Her soft fur smelled of smoke.

Lucky sneezed.

As the RV slowly drove away from the fires, Leela saw the forest change from thick, burning trees to piles of burnt wood.

"I think we are stuck here for a while," Dad said and parked the RV.

"It's so dark out!" Jaden yawned. "What time is it?"

"After dinnertime," Mom said as she stepped out of the RV to take pictures.

The flash from her camera was bright. There were no streetlights. The fires had stopped all the power. The only lights were brake lights from the cars ahead of them.

"I'm going to use my night vision goggles," Jaden said, pulling the straps around his head and turning on the blue light. "Cool! I can see people getting out of their cars."

WOOF! *WOOF!*

Lucky jumped at the door.

"What's wrong, Lucky?" Leela asked.

"Leela," Jaden said, "look at this . . ."

15

The Deer Dilemma

"**W**hat is it?" Leela asked as she put on her night vision goggles.

Jaden pointed out the window.

Four deer walked through a pile of burnt trees on the side of the road.

"They must be thirsty!" Leela said as she ran to the door. "We have to get them water!"

"Hold on!" Dad warned. "Remember what happened the last time you went to help an animal before you had a plan?"

Jaden rubbed his injured arm.

"There's no fire here," Leela pointed out. "The trees are all burned down."

BEEP! BEEP!

The baby deer looked up at the sound of a car horn honking. Drivers up and down the street flashed their headlights as a fire truck drove past them.

It was Fire Chief Fran and her team!

BEEP! BEEP!

The baby deer turned its head from side to side, then ran down the road, away from its family.

"Oh no! The beeping scared the deer!" Jaden cried.

Lucky whimpered.

"The buckets!" Leela remembered. "We can use the buckets we got from the farm in Kansas. Maybe some clean water will draw them back."

Mom nodded. "Let's fill them with water and lay them in a small path."

Dad turned on the hazard lights. Mom, Jaden, and Leela each poured water from the kitchen sink into a bucket and got out of the RV. They laid the buckets in a line on the side of the road before going back inside.

The Jackson family watched as three deer came and drank from the buckets.

"Little one, please come back," Leela whispered.

The RV was quiet.

"There!" Leela pointed.

Jaden and Leela watched as the baby deer bounced toward the buckets. It tipped its head and drank water next to its family.

"It came back!" Jaden said.

"Thank goodness there wasn't any fire and the deer were just thirsty. That could have been a disaster." Dad smiled.

The Jackson family cheered.

The buckets were a success!

16

Junior Firefighters

"Look!" Dad said as he pulled up to the emergency shelter.

Jaden, Leela, Lucky, and Mom yawned and stretched as they climbed out of the RV. It was almost ten p.m., but they had managed to get a few hours of sleep while Dad drove.

The air was smoky, but not as bad as in the forest. Leela looked up at the sky. She could see the stars.

"Come on!" Mom said. "It's just a quick stop to say goodbye to Fire Chief Fran!"

Up ahead was a big brick building with large doors.

"You made it!" said a familiar voice. Jaden and Leela turned to see Fire Chief Fran.

"Come inside," Fire Chief Fran said.

Inside was a kitchen, tables, chairs, beds, and even showers! People lined up to get safety kits.

"We helped pack those," Jaden said proudly.

Fire Chief Fran smiled. "You packed thirty safety kits. You are both now junior firefighters with Cal Fire." She handed out badges.

"So cool!" Jaden said.

"We can add these to our Disaster Squad Kits." Leela smiled.

"Great work, kiddos," Mom said.

Lucky barked.

Fire Chief Fran pinned a badge on Lucky's collar. "You were a great helper, too."

"What happens now?" Dad asked.

Fire Chief Fran sighed. "We have more air tankers, trucks, and supplies coming. For now, remember to put out campfires and stay safe during a wildfire."

Jaden and Leela waved goodbye as they climbed back into the RV to sleep for the night.

"We did it!" Jaden cheered, jumping on the couch.

Leela smiled. "I'm going to make my famous microwave s'mores. No fire needed!"

"Can we go to Laguna Beach tomorrow?" Jaden begged.

"Why not?" Dad smiled.

"It would be nice to have a break. This was one tough disaster," Mom said.

"It sure was!" Jaden said, pumping his fist in the air.

Just then, Mom's phone rang.

Everyone froze.

"Hello?" Mom answered. "Oh, really? Category two? We are on our way."

Jaden and Leela looked at each other. "Disaster," they said at the same time. "Jinx! Double jinx. Triple jinx!"

"Where are we headed?" Dad asked.

"Texas," Mom said, getting into the driver's seat. "It's midnight there and homes are flooding. The Gulf Coast is getting ready . . . for a hurricane."

About the Creators

Rekha S. Rajan is the author of several children's books including *Amazing Landmarks*, the This Is Music series, and *Can You Dance Like a Peacock?* She is a musician with a doctorate in education, and she works with educators nationwide to bring STEAM learning to the classroom. She lived in Northern California, where she saw the red sky, blazing wildfires, and brave firefighters. She now lives in Chicago with her husband, three children, three birds, a terrier named Brownie, and a German shepherd named Lucky.

Courtney Lovett is the illustrator of several children's books, including *Join the Club, Maggie Diaz*; *Santa's Gotta Go*; and *Basketball Dreams*, written by NBA all-star Chris Paul. She received her BFA in illustration and animation from UMBC. Utilizing both skill sets, she is driven to create stories that spark imagination and wonder in children. Today, she lives in her hometown in Maryland, where she illustrates books and teaches at a local art studio.

Wildfire Rescue
Questions & Activities

Look up the definition of a wildfire. What is the difference between a wildfire and a regular fire? How do wildfires start?

What things can you do to stay safe during a wildfire? How did Jaden and Leela help keep the community safe during the wildfires?

Have you gone camping? Look at the campfire checklist that Fire Chief Fran shared with Jaden and Leela. How did you help prevent wildfires?

 What animals did Leela and Jaden meet in this book? Which animal is your favorite?

Why was it dangerous for Jaden to try to save the bear cub? What should he have done instead?

Leela and Jaden travel across the country in their RV. Draw and label a map of where they travel! What states do they visit? What states do they drive through on their way to California?